Spaghetti Manners

By STEPHANIE CALMENSON
Illustrated by LISA McCUE KARSTEN

A GOLDEN BOOK • NEW YORK
Western Publishing Company, Inc., Racine, Wisconsin 53404

*B*lubble. *Blubble. Blubble.*

"Arthur, please stop blowing bubbles in your milk," said his mother.

"It tastes better when it's bubbly," Arthur said. But he stopped blowing the bubbles.

Arthur took a bite of his sandwich.

"Oh, Arthur!" said his mother. But before she could say any more, the phone rang.

"Grandpa is coming to dinner tonight," said
Mrs. Alligator when she hung up.

"Hurray!" said Arthur. "Can we have spaghetti?"

"That's a good idea. We can make it together," said
Mrs. Alligator. "I'll call you when it's time to start."

Arthur went to his room to play with his space set.

"Would you like spaghetti for dinner?" he asked his astronauts. "What? You say you don't want spaghetti floating around in your rocket ship? You say you would get all tangled up in spaghetti?"

Arthur laughed at the thought. "What a mess!" he said. Then he began the countdown.

"10...9...8...7...6..."

"Arthur," said Mrs. Alligator as she passed his room, "will you please try extra hard to remember your manners when Grandpa is here?"

"But there are so many," groaned Arthur. "How can I remember them all?"

"Maybe you can make some flash cards," suggested Mrs. Alligator.

When his mother had gone, Arthur finished the
countdown and sent his rocket ship into space. While
the ship was orbiting he thought about the flash
cards.

"I know," he said, "I'll make them look like
baseball cards, with pictures. That will be neat!"

Arthur got right to work.

"No blowing bubbles!" he said as he drew his first picture.

"My napkin belongs in my lap.

"I will not talk when my mouth is full."

Then he heard his mother calling, "It's time to cook the spaghetti, Arthur!"

In the kitchen, with a spaghetti box for his guitar, Arthur made up a spaghetti song:

"Oh, I like spaghetti.
That's why I sing this song.
Spaghetti is so skinny.
Spaghetti is so long!"

"That's a good song, Arthur," said Mrs. Alligator. "Now, would you find our big spaghetti pot?"

Bing! Bang! Bong! The pot was all the way at the back of the cabinet. Arthur had to make a lot of noise finding it.

As soon as it was quiet again, Arthur and his mommy heard the doorbell ring.

"Hi, Grandpa!" Arthur said, giving him a big hug.
"Guess what we're having for dinner—spaghetti!"
"That's great," said Grandpa. "I love spaghetti."
Then he handed Arthur a present.

"Thank you, Grandpa!" said Arthur. "This boat can meet my rocket when it lands in the ocean! Come, I'll show you."

Arthur and his grandpa played together until
Mrs. Alligator called them to dinner.

Then Arthur grabbed his flash cards and followed
his grandpa to the table.

As soon as he sat down Arthur placed his napkin in his lap. Then he took a drink of his milk and didn't blow one bubble.

"Would you like some bread?" asked Arthur's mother.

"Yes, please," Arthur said.

While Arthur was eating his bread Grandpa
asked, "How is school?"

Arthur pointed to his mouth to show that he had to
finish chewing. When he had swallowed the last
bit, he said, "School is fun!"

Finally Arthur's mother served the spaghetti. She filled Arthur's bowl to the top.

"Yum," said Arthur. He reached into the bowl and grabbed two big handfuls of spaghetti.

"Uh-oh," said Arthur when he saw the look on his
mother's face. He knew he shouldn't eat spaghetti with
his hands. Arthur looked at his flash cards, but they
were no help at all.

"Don't worry," said Arthur's grandpa. "You've had very good manners today. You've made me feel welcome. That's what manners are all about."
Grandpa gave Arthur a big hug.

"Now, I think you're going to like learning spaghetti manners," said Grandpa. "Watch what I do."

Grandpa put his fork into his spaghetti. He lifted the strands up high and put a big spoon underneath. Then he began to twirl the spaghetti till it made a neat little bundle.

"Open wide," said Grandpa. He popped the forkful of spaghetti into Arthur's mouth.

"Now you try it," said Arthur's mother.

Arthur put the fork into his spaghetti, his spoon underneath, and began to twirl it just like Grandpa had. While he was twirling the spaghetti he made up a new song:

'Oh, I like to twirl spaghetti
Because it is so long.
Twirling, curling, round it goes...

Then in a flash it's gone!"